For Suzi, with love

Colourful world

Colourful world

Mildenberger

Time for stories • Heft 8

Time for stories – Apps für das iPad

Der interaktive Einstieg in das englische Lektürelesen

www.time-for-stories.com

Erhältlich im App Store

Text und Idee: Bettina Erdmann
Illustrationen: Katrin Gaida
Layout und Satz: Elfe

Bestell-Nr. 5100-18 · ISBN 978-3-619-51180-8

www.mildenberger-verlag.de
E-Mail: info@mildenberger-verlag.de

Bezugsmöglichkeiten
Alle Titel des Mildenberger Verlags erhalten Sie unter: www.mildenberger-verlag.de oder im Buchhandel. Jede Buchhandlung kann alle Titel direkt über den Mildenberger Verlag beziehen. Ausnahmen kann es bei Titeln mit Lösungen geben: Hinweise hierzu finden Sie in unserem aktuellen Gesamtprogramm.

Auflage	8	7	6	5
Jahr	2018	2017	2016	2015

Druck: Herter Druck GmbH, 79341 Kenzingen
Gedruckt auf umweltfreundlichen Papieren

Funky is a little squirrel. She likes colours very much. So she likes wearing very colourful clothes: a green T-shirt, a red dress and yellow trainers.

Her home is in the trunk of a big old tree. You can find lots of things there: a yellow carpet, blue chairs, a red sofa and a green cupboard.

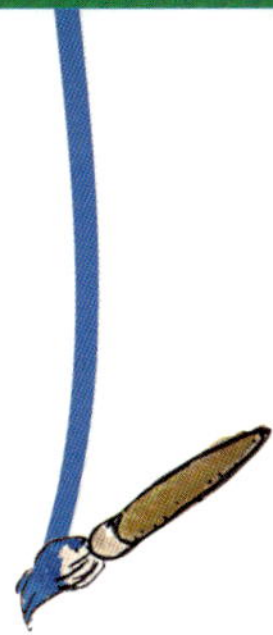

It is a warm day in August. Funky is playing with her friends. She likes the forest with all the trees very much. But there's one thing: All the trees are green and brown. And the ground is also just green and brown. "How boring!" Funky thinks. "If only there were other colours, too!"

Funky has got an idea. She gets some paint and starts painting the leaves of the trees: yellow, red and blue. Funky works very hard. In the afternoon a fox passes by.

"What the hell are you doing, crazy Funky?" the fox asks.

"You should be collecting nuts for the winter," he says. But Funky doesn't listen to the fox.

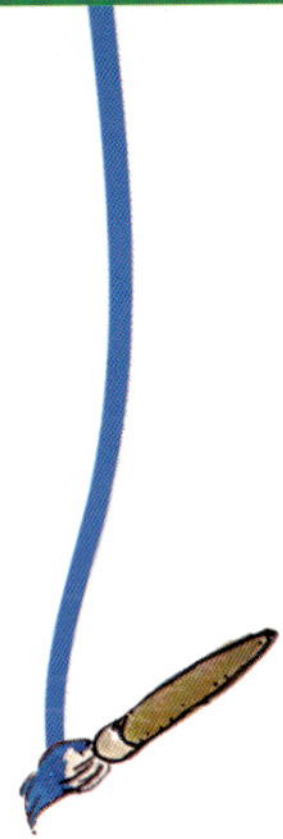

The other squirrels in the forest are very busy. They are collecting nuts and acorns and taking them home. They tell Funky about it but she isn't listening. She's busy, too.

Puh, finished! The forest is so colourful and Funky is very tired. She sleeps a little bit.

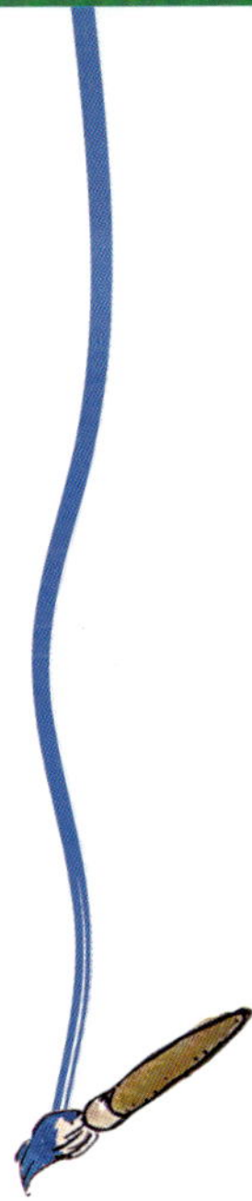

On the next day, when Funky wakes up and looks out of her tree, she can't believe what she sees: It's raining and the rain has washed all the paint off! All that work for nothing! No more colourful trees! Funky is very sad.

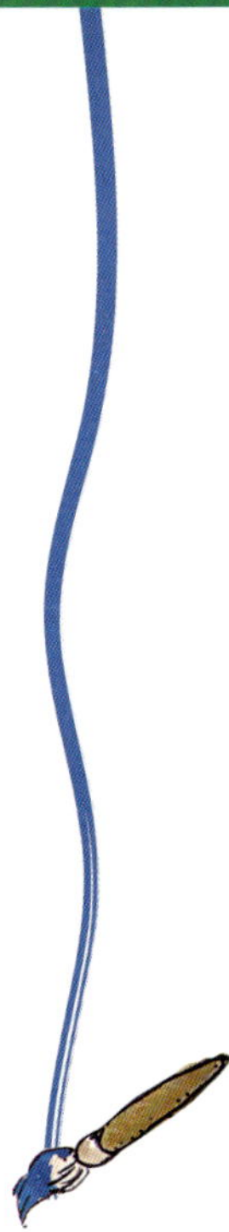

Some weeks later. It's a Sunday morning and Funky is at home. It starts getting colder at night now and the sun isn't warm anymore. Funky goes outside and – what can she see? All the leaves are red, yellow and brown! The sky is blue and the forest looks beautiful. Look at all the nice colours! It's autumn!

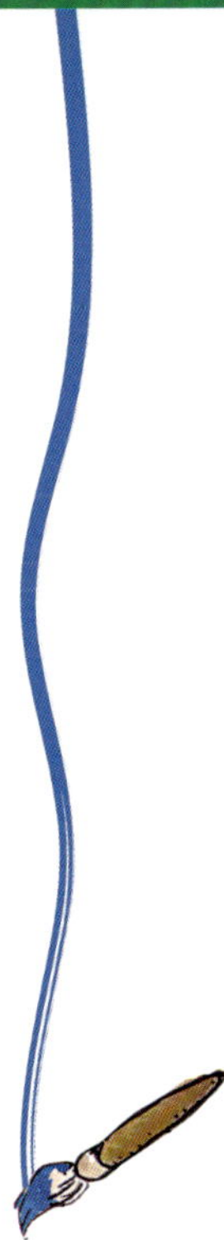

Now the days are getting colder
and colder, too. Winter is coming.
Funky has nothing to eat. She
hasn't collected any nuts. Oh no!
The fox was right. What now?
Someone is knocking at the door.
Funky opens it.

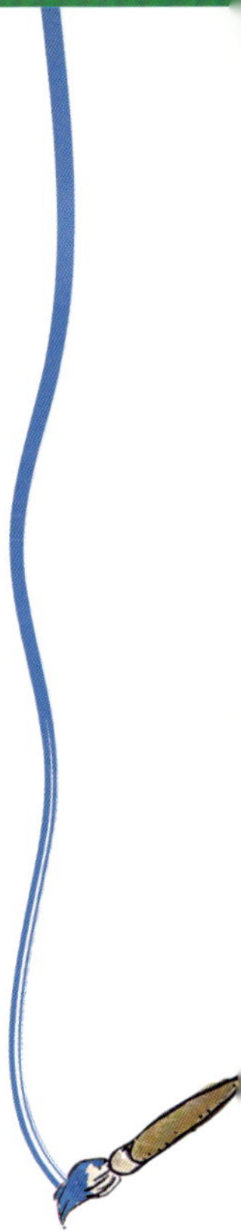

"Hello Funky!" say the three squirrels. They are Funky's friends. "We've brought you some nuts for the winter days. We know that you don't have any." "Come in!" Funky says. She is very happy. Nice to have good friends!

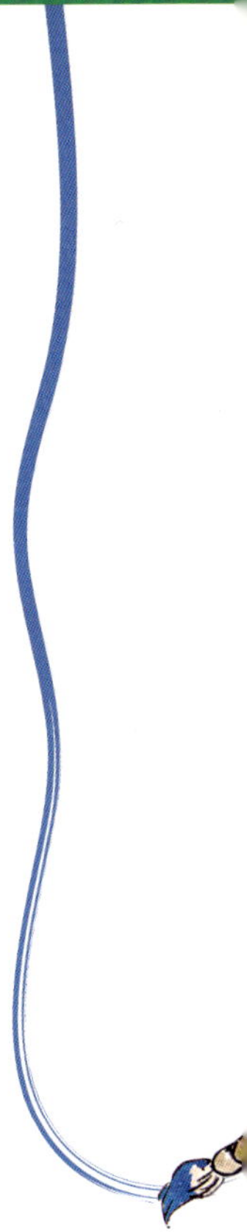

Time for stories

Frosty the snowman
Heft 1
VPE 5: 978-3-619-51110-5
VPE 25: 978-3-619-51111-2

Simon the sheep
Heft 2
VPE 5: 978-3-619-51120-4
VPE 25: 978-3-619-51121-1

At the fair
Heft 3
VPE 5: 978-3-619-51130-3
VPE 25: 978-3-619-51131-0

Happy Easter
Heft 4
VPE 5: 978-3-619-51140-2
VPE 25: 978-3-619-51141-9

A really big fish
Heft 5
VPE 5: 978-3-619-51150-1
VPE 25: 978-3-619-51151-8

Come on Arnie
Heft 6
VPE 5: 978-3-619-51160-0
VPE 25: 978-3-619-51161-7

Sea life
Heft 7
VPE 5: 978-3-619-51170-9
VPE 25: 978-3-619-51171-6

Colourful world
Heft 8
VPE 5: 978-3-619-51180-8
VPE 25: 978-3-619-51181-5

The little dragon
Heft 9
VPE 5: 978-3-619-51190-7
VPE 25: 978-3-619-51191-4

What a night
Heft 10
VPE 5: 978-3-619-51200-3
VPE 25: 978-3-619-51201-0

Heft 1 – 10 werden als Verpackungseinheit von 5 oder 25 Stück geliefert.

Bestellung im Set: Heft 1 – 10, je 1 Exemplar → Bestell-Nr. 4901-57
→ ISBN 978-3-619-49157-5

Bestellung im Set: Heft 1 – 10, je 5 Exemplare → Bestell-Nr. 4901-58
→ ISBN 978-3-619-49158-2

9 783619 511808

Bestell-Nr. 5100-18 · ISBN 978-3-619-51180-8